Halloween Surprise

Magical Midlife Series
By
Rose Bak

Table of Contents

Copyright

---

1. https://paperorpixels.com/

About This Book

He's just the demon to bring out her magic powers...

Raised as a "normal", it was easy for Jane to forget that she came from a long line of witches. Her mother always told her that the magic skipped their branch of the family tree but lately Jane's starting to wonder if that's really true. Her fortieth birthday is coming up on Halloween, and a lot of really weird things have been happening. A black cat starts following her around. She pictures her ex-boyfriend as a toad and suddenly he's croaking and eating flies. Oh, and there's the pesky little problem of accidentally starting fires with just her fingers.

When she goes back to her family's magical homestead to figure out what's happening, Jane ends up trapped in a closet with a guy who's tall, dark, handsome, and wearing horns.

Gabriel understands the stress of hiding one's true nature. The love child of a demon and a wolf shifter, he doesn't quite fit in either world. Until the night he runs into his fated mate at a Halloween party and things start making more sense for him. He just needs to convince his stubborn mate that they're meant to be... if only they could keep their hands off each other long enough to get to know each other first.

She thinks he's wearing a costume, but the truth is, Gabriel can't conceal his true nature from Jane. Is it her new magical powers? Or proof that she really is his fated mate?

"Halloween Surprise" is an instalove midlife romantic comedy with plenty of steam and a sweet happily ever after.

Join My Mailing List

Join Rose Bak's mailing list at bit.ly/rosebaknewsletter[2]. You'll get a free book and be the first to hear about all the latest releases, new freebies, and special sales.

---

2. https://storyoriginapp.com/giveaways/ba6caac0-d4f9-11ed-80b7-073007e1a152

Dedication

For everyone who wishes they could turn their horrible ex into a toad – or something worse. I get it, sister. We all do.

Jane

'Ribbit. Ribbit."

I looked around for the source of the noise. What the hell? There was a frog the size of a chihuahua sitting on my front porch, staring at me. Or maybe it was a toad, I wasn't quite sure about the difference. The frog-toad's eyes looked familiar though...

"Gerald? Is that you?" I wasn't sure how, but I was pretty sure this frog-toad was my ex-boyfriend.

"Ribbit. Ribbit." His tongue snuck out of his mouth, and he snatched a fly from the air.

"What in the world happened to you?"

"Ribbit."

"Well crap."

I pulled out my phone and called my cousin Pepper. Even though four years and several hundred miles separated us from each other, we'd always been close. We had a lot in common as the only two non-magical people in our generation of the family. Pepper's sister Cami was a witch, like their mother, and her sister Meri was a psychic, like their father.

But Pepper and I were just plain old "normals", as the other supernatural creatures called us. I'd always thought it was weird, but then again my mom was a normal despite the fact that her sister and mother were both powerful witches so I guessed it seemed logical that the magical genes could be recessive for some of us.

"Hey Jane, how goes it?" Pepper answered the phone on the second ring.

I lowered my voice, even though no one else was around.

"Weird stuff has been happening lately."

"What kind of weird stuff?"

"I was ranting about my cheating, lying scumbag ex..."

"Ribbit!"

"Yes, you Gerald," I hissed before turning my back to the frog-toad so I could focus on my call. "Anyway, I was saying yesterday that I hoped he turned into a big fat toad and, well, there's a big fat toad on my porch with Gerald's eyes."

"Are you sure it's a toad?" she asked, as usual focusing on the most important thing in any conversation.

"Frog, toad, I don't know. Whatever it is, it's really big and eating flies."

"Probably a frog then."

I sighed deeply. "The point is, I wished he was a frog, then he showed up as a frog."

"Oh. Huh."

"Yeah. And that's not all. There's this black cat that's been following me around all week and I know this is insane, but I swear I can tell what it's thinking. Then a couple of days ago I was super annoyed because I couldn't find any matches to light the fireplace and I, well, I started a fire with my fingers. Then I did it again yesterday to start the grill."

"Holy crap. Cami and my mom can start fires like that. It's super cool."

"Yeah, but Cami and your mom are witches, remember?"

I plopped on the porch swing while Froggie Gerald continued to stare at me balefully.

"The magic skipped me though, so that doesn't make sense."

My mother had explained it all to me several times. Even though we came from a magical family, sometimes a branch of the family tree turned out normal, like from recessive genes or something. That's why my mom and I didn't have any powers. At least I always thought I didn't have any powers...

"Do you think the magic is latent or something?" Pepper asked excitedly. "Maybe that means I'll get some powers in a couple of years too when I turn forty like you."

Pepper had always been bitter about not having powers. Since I'd been raised in the human world, it hadn't bothered me as much.

"I have no idea. But I probably need to fix Gerald somehow. I can't leave him like this."

"Ribbit!"

"Why don't you come to Colorado?" Pepper suggested. "You can stay at Rosewater Manor with us. We can do something fun for your birthday and then we'll see if we can figure out what to do about your froggie friend."

"Maybe your mom can change him back?"

"She and Dad are traveling, but I'm sure Cami would be willing to help. If she doesn't mess it up…"

Pepper's sister wasn't the best witch. She'd once done a love spell for Pepper and wound up making the guy fall in love with herself instead. Needless to say, Pepper had been annoyed.

"If Cami can't do it, we'll call my mom and ask her to come back and help."

"Okay, that sounds like a good plan. I'll drive up tomorrow."

"See you then."

The next morning, I packed up my car to make the seven hour drive to Colorado from my home in Amarillo. My cousins lived south of Denver in an area that was mostly forest and small towns filled with supernatural residents. Not that most humans knew that. They liked to pretend that the supernatural world didn't exist, and most supes were glad to let them believe that.

I packed Gerald into a cat carrier to keep him from being thrown around in the car when I drove the curvy mountain roads. I was just about to get in the car when the black cat appeared out of nowhere.

"Meow."

The creature gave me a haughty look as she leapt into the car and settled into the passenger seat. Apparently she was coming with me.

"Fine, you can come with us, but stay on the seat so you don't go through the window if I brake unexpectedly."

"Meow."

Seven hours later I pulled into the drive of Rosewater Manor, my family's historical homestead. Rosewaters had lived there for generations, except for my mother. She'd gone to college in Texas, met my father, and other than brief visits hadn't been back since. I stepped out of the car, smelling the fresh scent of the nearby forest, and immediately felt better than I had in weeks. The air around me seemed to vibrate with magic, I realized with a start. I'd never felt that any other time I'd visited.

My cousin Pepper burst out of the house, pulling me into a tight hug. Like me, she had brown hair, brown eyes, and a little more curves than either of us would prefer.

"Jane, I'm so glad to see you!"

I opened the door, releasing the cat, then Pepper reached in and grabbed the cat carrier holding Gerald. Raising it up to her face, she gave Gerald a wink through the bars of the carrier door.

"Don't worry, we'll figure this out."

I hoped she was right.

Gabriel

"Come on Gabe, it's going to be a great party."

"I don't even know the guy, besides, I'm not really in a party mood," I said, looking at my brother Duncan. Well, half-brother anyway.

I studied him, thinking for not the first time that no one would doubt we were brothers. We were both tall and broad, with dark hair, dark eyes, and scruff that pretty much grew back five minutes after we shaved. My little brother was about an inch taller and probably had another twenty pounds of muscle compared to me, but that was the only difference between us.

"Preston's my best friend, you're going to have to meet him sooner or later anyway. Why not at a costume party."

Even though we were in our late thirties, I'd only met my brother about a year ago. My mother had been tight-lipped about my father's identity my entire life, revealing nothing no matter how much I'd tried to pump her for information. She'd raised me by herself in the same demon neighborhood where she'd grown up. My father had never been in the picture—all I knew was that he was a wolf shifter, and I only knew that once I started wolfing out when I was an angry adolescent. My mother was a demon – the good kind, don't worry – and she kept my father's secret to the grave.

Although she'd raised me as a demon, Mom at least she had the courtesy to leave the details in a letter that her lawyer gave me when he read the will after her death from cancer. The letter, which was dated about six months before she died, answered a lot of questions I'd had all my life.

Gabe,

I promised your father I would go to my grave with this secret, and I did. Here's what you need to know about your birth. Your father and I met at a party in college. It was a shifter party, so the alcohol was stronger than the humans drink and, well, one thing led to another and a few months later I realized I was pregnant. I went searching for your father to tell him about you and learned that he had found his fated mate and married her after we were together. We agreed not to upset his mate, especially since she was pregnant. As you know, my family had money, so I didn't need child support from him. Instead, your father left a sizable sum in a trust for you to be given to you after my death – or his, whichever came first. I kept him up to date over the years about you and your life, so please don't think he wasn't interested in you. By the time you and Duncan's other child were old enough to understand what had happened, we decided to keep the status quo since you were both doing well. Your father is Duncan Fields Sr., and he lives in Greysden, Colorado. If you want to see him now that I've passed on, he's ready for that and very eager to finally meet you. Please don't be angry with me, I did what I thought was best for you, always. I love you with all my heart. Mom"

After taking care of my mother's estate, I'd headed to Colorado where I met my father and stepmother. Honestly, that had gone better than I'd expected, and to my complete surprise, they'd welcomed me into their family. It turned out that I loved Colorado, so I decided to stay in the area. With my mom dead, there wasn't a lot holding me in New Jersey anyway.

The truth was, I'd never really felt like I fit in anywhere until I came to Greysden. Half shifter, half demon, it was a weird combination. I looked like a "normal" when I was in my human form, but it was really just a glamor. All the demons had it. It hid our demon features from anyone who wasn't supernatural, at least until I got really angry. Then my wolf side would take over and I'd grow fur and fangs to go along with my demon horns. I'd never seen myself like that – it's not like I went looking for a mirror during a shift – but I understood that I looked terrifying. I didn't mind that.

What I did mind was never feeling like I fit in anywhere. I wasn't quite human, wasn't a full demon, and wasn't a full shifter. I could live in one of three worlds, but I'd fit in nowhere until I came to Colorado.

Fortunately, everyone in Greysden was a little weird. We had witches, wolves, bears, even some badger shifters, and lots and lots of mixed species hybrids. I wasn't even the weirdest hybrid in town. It felt good to not be the weirdo.

A few months after I relocated, my brother Duncan Jr. moved back to Greysden with his boss, billionaire CEO Preston Rutherford. The guy was a 'normal' until he was turned into a shifter by rogue wolves. Duncan had encouraged Preston to move someplace where he could explore his new shifter abilities, and they'd settled on Greysden. I was glad they did. I was glad he was close. Duncan and I had immediately hit it off, and now he was one of my best friends.

"Where is this party, anyway?" I asked my brother.

"Preston rented the Greysden Mansion. It's this huge old Victorian mansion that they rent out for parties and weddings. It's a great site. Very spooky for a Halloween event."

"What'll I wear?" I asked.

Duncan rolled his eyes. "It's a Halloween party, man. Just go in your demon form and have some fun."

A few days later I rolled up to the Greysden Mansion in my SUV. I was wearing faded denim jeans and a black leather jacket with no shirt, showing off the demon markings that most humans would mistake for tattoos. I also lowered the glamor so the humans could see my horns.

Speaking of horns, as soon as I got out of the car, they started to throb. That was weird, they usually only did that when I was turned on. Then my dick twitched, getting in on the action. What the hell?

I headed into the party, relieved to see my brother as soon as I walked in. He was Preston's chief of security as well as his best friend, but tonight he was dressed up like a vampire, with fake teeth and a black cape.

"I take it you're a movie vampire?" I asked sarcastically.

"Of course," Duncan said, giving me a one armed hug. "We both know real vampires wouldn't be caught dead looking like this."

"Caught dead?" I laughed. "They already are dead."

"You know what I mean."

Suddenly I heard a voice in my head. *Mine! Mate! Mate!*

My brother watched me carefully. "What is it?"

"It's my wolf. He's super agitated. He doesn't usually talk, he just sends me images, but he seems to be talking now. At least I hope it's him, otherwise I'm just hearing voices in my head."

"What's he saying?" Duncan asked.

"It doesn't make sense. He keeps saying 'mine' and 'mate' and demanding we go find someone," I grunted. "I'm having a hard time holding him back."

Duncan gave me a big smile. "Well congratulations big brother, it looks like you've finally found your mate."

"Huh?"

"Oh yeah, I forgot you grew up among the demons. Every shifter has a fated mate, one person who's the perfect match for them. Once your inner animal identifies his mate, he won't rest until you mate her and mark her as yours forever. Or him, no judgement here."

"Wait, that mate stuff is true? I thought that was just a legend or something."

I winced as my wolf scratched at my insides and resumed his demands that we find our mate.

"Oh, it's true. You'd better find her before you wolf out. Even in Greysden it's frowned upon to shift in the middle of a party."

Jane

"This costume is ridiculous. Forty-year-old women shouldn't dress like this!"

I adjusted the neckline of the tiny little nurse costume that my cousin had convinced me to wear. Unfortunately, that just made the hemline rise up my thighs even more.

"No way, it's cute." Pepper looked me over critically. "You've got the big boobs to make it work."

We both looked up as a voice growled, "Mine!"

A hot guy was striding towards us, his eyes fixed on me in the most unsettling way. I'd estimate he was a hair over six feet tall, with short dark hair and dark eyes that seemed to be glowing red in the low light of the room. His face was weathered but handsome, with one of those circle beard things, where there was dark scruff surrounding his mouth and chin, but it didn't go all the way up his jaw.

He was wearing a leather jacket without a shirt, showing wide shoulders, a toned chest covered with tattoos, and ridged abs that made my mouth water. He looked big and dark and the tiniest bit dangerous. Maybe it was the demon horns he was wearing as part of his costume.

He stopped in front of me, his face looking shell-shocked. "Mate!"

"Oh for Goddess sake, I can't believe this is happening again."

I tore my gaze away from the man to look at my cousin. "What are you talking about, Pepper?"

"I'm like a good luck charm for shifters finding their fated mate. Meanwhile I'm destined to be alone." She sighed deeply. "I'll just leave you to it and catch up with you later."

"What? Wait!"

Pepper scampered off, leaving us alone.

"Who are you?" I asked the man. I had the strongest urge to push him to the ground and rub myself all over him.

"Gabriel."

Our eyes met and held as the air between us vibrated with...something. I couldn't define it. It was like a combination of heat and, dare I say it? Magic.

I don't know what got into me, but I felt compelled to be alone with him. Right now. I grabbed his wrist, feeling a frisson of sensation, almost like he was electrified or something, as I tugged him behind me. I pulled him down the hallway, trying a couple of doors before I found one that was unlocked. A utility closet.

Closing us inside, I leaned against the door, somehow desperate to keep him from leaving.

"Who are you?" I asked again, feeling entranced. Was he a warlock or something? I didn't feel like myself at all.

"Your future."

I would have laughed at the corny line, but before I could take my next breath he cupped my cheeks in his palms and pressed his lips against mine. My body's reaction was instantaneous. My nipples hardened and I felt a rush of arousal flood my core. I didn't know what was happening, but I was damn well going to enjoy it.

I slid my hands under his jacket to wrap around his waist and he shuddered a little at my touch. I licked along the seam of his lips, demanding entrance, and when he parted his lips I shoved my tongue in to explore his mouth. I scarcely recognized myself—I'd never been aggressive with a man like this before.

Gabriel groaned and took over, sucking my tongue further into his mouth and lowering his hands to rub my breasts through the thin fabric of my costume.

Everything felt frantic: our mouths, our hands, our very breath – it was all rushed, like it was the end of the world and we needed to fit in one last fuck before the apocalypse. I'd never felt this desperate for a guy in my entire life.

I dropped my hands to his waist, unsnapping his jeans and pulling down the zipper. He was commando, and his cock jumped out right into my hand. He growled as I gave him a few firm pumps. He felt so good in hand, like silk over hard steel, with a bead of pre-cum glistening at the tip.

I shivered as Gabriel nipped along my jaw and down the side of my neck to the top of my shoulder, soothing each tiny bite with a swipe of his tongue.

He pulled away and dropped to his knees, pulling my sodden panties down on the way. I kicked them off as he shoved my skirt up to my waist and pressed a kiss right at my apex. The gesture was both sweet and arousing.

"Mine," he grumbled again before sliding his rough tongue through my wet folds.

"Oh God," I whined, grabbing his short hair to direct him where I needed him most.

Gabriel tapped his tongue along my clit then sucked it between his lips, alternating between licking and tapping and sucking. I made a keening noise and grabbed onto his horns, surprised when they didn't fall off.

"These things are on pretty tight," I panted.

I slid my fingers up and down the horns, noting that they felt just like the horns on my neighbor's pet goats. It was weird, but I was too focused on what Gabriel was doing with his magical tongue to think too much about it.

Gabriel surged to his feet again, lifting me up with hands gripped behind either thigh. I leaned against the door, wrapping my thighs around his waist, and rolling my hips until his cock slid between my folds. Staring into my eyes, he pushed into me, stretching me wide as he bottomed out in my channel with one long thrust. We both groaned loudly, pausing as my body adjusted.

"You're fucking perfect, Mate," he bit out.

With a deep growl, he started pounding into me. It was hard and rough and perfect. I braced my hands on his shoulders and pushed against the door so I could meet him thrust for thrust. The door rattled behind me with the force of our movement, and it occurred to me that anyone walking by would know what we were doing in here. It only heightened my excitement.

Gabriel reached between us, pinching my clit, and I shuddered as the strongest orgasm I'd had in my life rolled through my body. He was right behind me, his motions becoming erratic as he thrusted into me a few more times, pushing so roughly that my head bounced against the surface of the door. I felt the heat of his seed releasing in me just as he lowered his mouth and bit my shoulder so hard he broke the skin.

It was painful and erotic and enough to pull another orgasm out of me. I swear I left my body for a few minutes, and when I returned to consciousness Gabriel was leaning against me, holding me up against the door with his body weight as he licked the blood of the wound he'd left on my shoulder. It should have been gross, but somehow it felt perfect.

When he finally stepped back, my feet slid to the floor, legs unsteady.

"Well," I said shakily. "That was...something."

I readjusted my dress and looked around until I found my panties on the floor. They were soaked. Grimacing, I shoved them into my purse.

Gabriel was leaning against a shelf full of cleaning products, looking as wrecked as I felt. What the hell had just happened?

"Thanks for giving me a little birthday gift," I said, striving to keep my tone casual. I hadn't had a lot of casual hook-ups, but I knew how this went. No sense being clingy, even if this was the best sex I'd ever had. "Maybe I'll see you around."

"Wait."

"Sorry, I've got to go."

I gripped the door handle and pulled, swearing when nothing happened.

"What?" he asked, still looking totally out of it. I wondered if I'd fucked the sense right out of him. I kind of liked the idea that I could have that much effect on a guy who looked like that.

"We're locked in."

"Someone will come by eventually," he said, giving me a sultry look that made more moisture run down my thighs.

I stalked closer. "I have an idea how we can pass the time."

Gabriel

After pushing me to the floor and riding me until we were both shouting out with the intensity of our simultaneous orgasms, my mate was laying on top of me, playing with my chest hair.

The woman was a vision with her curvy body, long brown hair, and a heart-shaped face that held an expression of pure satisfaction. At least until I opened my big, fat mouth.

"What's your name, Mate?" I asked.

I could see the exact moment that she started to realize the enormity of what had just happened between us. She stiffened above me, brown eyes narrowing to slits.

"Oh my God! We just fucked – twice—and you don't even know my name? What the hell am I doing?"

She leapt up to standing, adjusting the sexy nurse costume she was wearing and covering all of my favorite parts of her body.

"I forgot to ask," I said lamely. "We were a little busy."

That just made her angrier. She slapped the door with her palm, hard enough to make the door shake, and hissed, "Open, you stupid door!"

The air glimmered with magic and the door burst open, surprising both of us.

"Are you a witch?" I asked curiously.

"No."

"Wait, don't go."

She hightailed it out of the room while I lay on the floor, wondering what the hell had just happened. My wolf was growling at me to go after her, but I took a few minutes to regroup, knowing enough of the mate lore to understand that now that I'd found her, I'd be able to track her by scent.

At least I was pretty sure about that. Crap, what if that was just a rumor? It wasn't like demons had that skill. I leapt to my feet and raced out the door, running into my brother as I exited the closet.

"What happened?" Duncan asked. "Did you find your mate?"

He sniffed, then gave me a smile. "Never mind, I can smell that you did. Where is my future sister-in-law?"

"She took off," I admitted sheepishly.

"What happened?" he asked. "You couldn't get her over the finish line?"

"I got her over the finish line," I snapped. "She ran away afterwards. Also, um, I don't know what came over me, but I kind of bit her."

"You gave her a mate mark without her consent?" Duncan asked shrewdly. "That's a big no-no."

"I was raised as a demon, remember? Dealing with a pushy wolf is new for me. He was always pretty quiet unless I got angry or something, but now tonight suddenly he's talking, ordering me around, and biting women we just met. He's out of control."

"How do I always get stuck being the wolf shifter trainer?" Duncan mused. "Much have you to learn about your wolf side brother," he continued in a terrible Yoda impression.

"Are you just going to joke around, or can you actually help me?" I griped.

"Okay, okay, well the good news is that I know the woman your mate was with." At my raised eyebrows he added, "Your mate was with Pepper, whose sister is Preston's mate. Let's find her and see what she knows about your mate."

I followed Duncan to a couple that was practically climbing each other in the corner of the room.

"Preston. Meri. I'd like to introduce you to my brother, Gabriel."

The couple split apart, giving me friendly smiles.

"Hi Gabriel, I'm Meri," the younger woman said. She was short and curvy and dressed like a fairy. Something about her made me like her immediately. "This is my boyfriend—," she paused as Preston growled, "I mean, my *mate* Preston."

"Gabriel, great to finally meet you," Preston added, reaching out to shake my hand. He was dressed like a wizard and wearing shoes that I'd bet cost more than my car.

"Hey Meri, do you know who that woman was that came to the party with Pepper?" Duncan asked. "She was dressed like a nurse."

"Yeah, that was our cousin Jane. She's visiting from Texas, why?" Her eyes widened. "Do you like her, Duncan? Is she your mate?"

I growled involuntarily and Meri stared at me. "Why are your eyes red? I've never seen a shifter with red eyes."

When I didn't answer Duncan explained, "He's half demon. And he's the one who is Jane's mate, not me. Do you know where your cousin went?"

"She and Pepper just left. They're probably heading back to Rosewater Manor," Meri said. "Jane is staying with us for a few days while she figures out...some things."

I started to leave but Meri grabbed my arm. "Maybe wait until morning to go over there. It's after midnight. They're probably in bed."

Suddenly she gasped and gripped her head, the fingers on my arm tightening almost painfully. "You have a flat tire."

"Huh?"

"You ran over a nail, your back tire is flat now."

I looked at Duncan in confusion. "She's a psychic," he explained.

I shook my head. "This is the most fascinating little town."

"Greysden is special," Duncan confirmed. "Come on, I'll help you put on your spare."

Jane

"Ribbit!"

"Look Gerald I'm sorry, but I have no clue how to turn you back. And since my cousin Cami can't figure it out either, we're just going to need to wait for my Aunt Sage to come back from her trip."

"Are you talking to a frog, Jane?"

I jumped as I heard the deep voice behind me. I'd been so focused on Gerald that I hadn't heard Gabriel walk up. I turned around slowly, taking in his dark hair, damp from the shower, and the faded jeans and blue tee-shirt that hugged his muscles like a second skin. One look at the sexy scruff beard thing he had going on and my core was clenching with need.

"What are you doing here?" I asked. I really wanted to suggest that he fuck me right here on my family's porch, but I resisted that urge.

"I came to see you, Jane. I think we should talk, Jane."

I rolled my eyes at the deliberate way he said my name.

"Yeah, yeah, I get it, someone told you my name. Now what do you want?"

Before he could answer, the black cat that had been following me around pranced out of the house, wrapping his furry body around Gabriel's legs. Lucky cat.

"Who's this?" Gabriel asked, leaning down to stroke the cat's head. He purred happily. The cat, not Gabriel.

"My Familiar, apparently."

"What's that?"

"It's kind of like an animal spiritual guide for witches," I responded. "Except I'm not a witch."

The cat hissed angrily, and Gabriel chuckled. "It would appear your Familiar disagrees."

"Why are you here again?"

"I was hoping we could talk. Could we take a walk or something? It's a beautiful day."

He gave me a pleading look that I couldn't resist. The truth was, I was dying to spend more time with him, even if it was a bad idea. I wasn't sure why it was a bad idea, but it really seemed like it should be.

"Fine."

I picked up Gerald and set him inside of the house and hollered, "Pepper, I'm going to take a walk."

I stalked down the long driveway towards the road, Gabriel walking beside me.

"Well? What did you want to talk to me about?"

I could hear the belligerent tone in my voice. Gabriel probably didn't deserve that, but I couldn't help it. My life was already being upended enough with whatever was happening with my new powers, I didn't need to deal with a clingy one night stand on top of everything else. I ignored the voice in my head that insisted Gabriel was way more than a one night stand.

"I'm sorry I bit you," he said suddenly. "I didn't realize it was frowned upon."

My hand automatically went to the rapidly healing wound on my shoulder. It tingled when I touched it, like it was some kind of erogenous zone.

"I guess I don't mind a little biting in the heat of the moment," I said softly.

"It wasn't a little biting. It's a mate bite."

"It's a what now?"

"It's a mate bite. It's kind of like a shifter marriage. It binds us together for the rest of our lives."

His voice was so casual and pragmatic that it took a few seconds for his words to sink in. I stopped dead and whipped around to face him.

"WHAT?!?!?"

"We're kind of married now," he said sheepishly. "I haven't had a lot of experience as a shifter, I honestly didn't realize the implications of biting you or I would've tried harder to hold my wolf back. Not that I'm sorry I did it, I'm just sorry I didn't get your consent. But we can't take it back. You have a husband now."

He ran his hand through his hair, drawing my attention to the horns that were still perched on his head.

"Why the hell are you still in costume?"

"Huh?"

"The horns, why are you still wearing them? Halloween is over."

He stopped walking and turned to study me carefully. "You can see my horns?"

"Yeah."

He lifted his shirt, revealing washboard abs that made me want to throw him to the ground and lick every inch of his body. "Can you see my markings too?"

Good lord, this guy was nuts.

"Your tattoos? Of course, I can. I have eyes don't I?" I snapped.

"Wow, it's really true."

I stared at him for a long moment before asking, "What's true?"

"You and I are fated to be together for all time."

"Because I reminded you that you're still wearing your Halloween costume? Because if so, I have to tell you, your standards for mates seems kind of low. And also, I'm not interested in whatever you think this is."

Gabriel grabbed my hand, and I tried not to notice the way it made my skin vibrate with attraction. I also ignored the way my nipples perked up happily.

"You don't understand. I'm a demon."

"I thought you were a shifter."

"I'm half demon and half shifter," he explained.

"And you're fully crazy."

I stalked away, and he followed me with a growl that dampened my panties. Gabriel jumped in front of me and before I knew what was happening, he threw me over his shoulder and stomped into the wood that lined the road.

"What are you doing?" I asked, pounding on his back. It was like pounding on a rock. "Answer me, damn it."

"Be quiet."

His big hand came down on my ass in a sharp slap, and I gasped in outrage. Of all the nerve...and also, why did I like that?

He walked for at least three minutes before setting me down in a clearing. As soon as my feet hit the ground, I started walking away again.

"Please Jane, wait."

I couldn't say why, but something in his voice made me stop walking and turn back to face him. He motioned towards a large boulder lodged between two giant trees. "I'm doing a shitty job of explaining. Can we sit for a minute and talk? I swear I'll explain everything."

My aggrieved sigh filled the silent space. "You've got five minutes and then I'm out of here."

Gabriel

I sat on the large boulder and patted the space beside me. To my surprise, Jane sat next to me without a complaint. I turned sideways to get a better look at her. She was wearing yoga pants, gym shoes, and a faded sweatshirt with another top peeking out from beneath the hemline. Her chocolate brown hair was pulled up in a messy bun. With her face free of make-up, her eyes looked huge against the white of her skin.

It was nice here in the forest, the tall trees filtering the sun and making the air fresh and clean, a nice change from the pollution I'd breathed in when I lived in New Jersey.

"My mom was a demon," I started. "She had a short-lived affair with a wolf shifter, but they broke up before she realized she was pregnant. Turns out that after he and my mom split, my father found his true mate, and his mate was also pregnant. My father's mate had a rough pregnancy and with them being newly mated, my parents decided to keep me a secret to avoid upsetting his mate."

Jane didn't comment, just stared into space, but I could tell that she was listening.

"I was raised in the demon world and learned their ways, but I knew I was part wolf too, even if I didn't understand what that meant. My wolf was mostly dormant unless I was upset about something, and my demon side was the dominant one. But I'd always wondered about who my father was and where he lived. When my mother died, she left behind information on my father was and how to find him. He lives in Greysden, so I came out to Colorado to meet him and his mate. That's when I learned about my brother Duncan."

"Duncan is your brother?" she asked curiously. "The big guy who's friends with Meri's mate?"

"Yeah. I had no idea that I had a brother. He's six months younger than me."

"Weird."

"When I saw you last night, it was like you woke my wolf up. He got a little, um, overexcited after we um, you know, so he bit you. I'd heard about the mate bite, but I thought it was some shifter fairy tale until you left, and Duncan explained that it's real."

"What's this got to do with your Halloween costume?" she asked in confusion.

"It's not a costume. Those are my demon horns. I was born with them, but all demons have the ability to put up a glamor, so only other demons can see their true nature. Or soul mates."

She jerked at the word. "Your demon side thinks I'm your soul mate and your wolf thinks I'm your fated mate, do I have that right?"

"Yeah."

She didn't look as surprised by all this as I thought she would be, making me wonder how much of the mate pull she was feeling. I wasn't sure how it affected witches, but I'd heard that humans could feel it for sure, just not as strongly as supernaturals.

"This is a lot to take in," Jane said softly. "Especially with whatever's going on with me right now."

"What do you mean?"

"I grew up thinking I was a 'normal', but lately witchy things have been happening, like last night when I magicked the door open. I'm not sure how this could be happening, but I seem to be developing powers. I was hoping coming to see my family would help me figure out what's happening. Meeting you, well, it's a complication."

She finally turned to face me, her brown eyes burning. I took her hand, threading my fingers through hers. A current ran between us everywhere that our skin touched.

I couldn't say who moved first, but suddenly we were kissing. My wolf hummed happily as I deepened the kiss, sweeping my tongue into her mouth. I shifted my weight, gently pushing Jane down onto her back on the boulder before laying on top of her. I balanced my weight on my forearms and rolled my pelvis into hers as I continued to kiss her.

When we finally parted I gasped, "I want you Jane."

"Dammit." That was all she said before she grabbed my head and pulled me down for another kiss.

Her hands slid between us, unzipping my zipper, and I rolled to the side so I could free my cock and rip her yoga pants and underwear down her legs.

"Mate! You're so beautiful."

My voice was more wolf than human as I moved between her legs, shoving my shoulders between them to open her wide for me. Her pussy was pink and already glistening with arousal, and I couldn't resist taking a taste.

"Ahh!" Jane's hips lifted as I ran my tongue between her folds. I shifted, bringing her legs over my shoulders as I focused my attention on her clit. I swept around it with my tongue, over and over, never getting quite close enough to get her off. Jane gripped my hair, pulling me to where she wanted me.

I lifted my head, giving her a wicked smile. "Feeling impatient, little mate?"

When she just glared at me I lowered my head again, this time tapping my tongue directly against the swollen bundle of nerves near the junction of her legs. My cock was pressed painfully against the boulder we lay on, but I wanted to get her off first. Needed to get her off first. I'd never felt this intense desire to satisfy my partner before. But then again, I hadn't had a mate before.

When I sucked her clit between my lips and bit down, giving her just the tip of my wolf fangs, she came apart, shaking and shuddering as she moaned my name. It was beautiful.

Before she even caught her breath I moved up her body, sliding skin against skin. Jane bent her knees, opening herself wide as I notched my cock against her opening. She was already dripping wet from her orgasm, so I just shoved my cock inside of her with one long stroke, causing us both to groan.

"I feel so full," she moaned.

"Is it too much?"

Her inner muscles tightened around my cock as if to keep me inside of her. "Never."

Our eyes met and held as I began a steady rhythm, pumping in and out of her in long strokes. She raised her hips to meet me with each thrust.

"Your eyes," she gasped. "They glow red when you're inside me."

"My demon side wants you as much as my wolf side," I replied, increasing my pace.

Jane reached up to grab my horns and I growled deep in my throat.

"Does it hurt when I touch them?" she asked, dropping her hands immediately. Her face was etched with concern.

"No," I grunted, words becoming more difficult. "Erogenous zone."

Her eyes widened but she didn't reply, instead moving her hands back to stroke my horns. They were throbbing in time with my cock. Her grip tightened as a second orgasm wracked her body, making her shudder beneath me, mouth open in a silent scream. I was right behind her, groaning again as I reached my own release, shooting my seed deep inside her as my wolf howled happily in my mind.

I rolled us to our sides as I collapsed, exhausted from the intensity of what had just happened. I wondered idly if it would be like this every time we were together.

And then she screamed.

Jane

The creature stalking towards us stopped dead at the sound of my scream, its massive head tilted to the side like it was trying to figure out what happened. In a flash Gabriel had his body in front of mine and despite every feminist tendency I had, I appreciated the protective gesture.

"What the fuck is that?" I whispered. "It looks like a prehistoric pig."

"It's a wild boar," Gabriel responded, just as quietly. "A real one, not a shifter."

It was a good clarification. In this part of Colorado, a seemingly wild animal was more likely to be a shape shifter than an actual animal.

"What's he doing this far north?" I mused. I was pretty sure wild boars normally lived in warmer climates.

"No clue."

I met the boar's eyes. He looked a little crazy. Was I supposed to assert dominance or play dead? I had no idea. The creature bared its teeth, and I wondered if boars could get rabies. Damn it, I hated getting shots. Suddenly the wild boar made a loud snorting noise and started rushing towards us again.

I didn't think, I just threw up my hand in front of Gabriel's body protectively and yelled, "Get back!"

The air around my hand shimmered and to my shock, the boar lifted up and went flying backwards, landing on his back before twisting to his feet. The creature seemed stunned as it gave us one last look and then lumbered off into the woods as if he were being chased.

"Nice job," Gabriel looked impressed as he jumped off the bolder and started gathering up our clothes. "I didn't know you could do that."

"Neither did I."

We both got dressed and headed back towards the road to Rosewater Manor, taking the long way around through the woods while walking hand in hand and talking softly. It was...nice.

After a few minutes, Gabriel asked, "Can you tell me more about the witchcraft thing? I mean, if you don't mind."

"Even though I was raised as a 'normal', the last month or so strange things are happening to me. The cat appeared and we seem to be able to read each other's thoughts. I've started fires with my fingers a couple of times. Oh, and I somehow turned my idiot ex-boyfriend into a toad and that's just what happened before I got to Greysden," I explained. "It's weird because when my cousin Pepper and I were kids, we tried everything we could think of to activate any latent magic powers, with no luck. I don't understand what's happening, or why it's happening now."

"Has anything changed in your life recently?" he asked.

"Nothing really. Other than I turned forty yesterday. Oh, and my mother got married and moved to Florida a few months ago," I responded. "I'm hoping my Aunt Sage gets here soon. She's a badass witch. If anyone can figure out what's going on, it's her."

When we got back to Rosewater Manor, both the cat and froggie Gerald were waiting for me on the porch.

"Ribbit!" Gerald shifted his toad body in between my feet and Gabriel's, glaring at Gabriel's ankles. I almost stepped on him.

"Knock it off Gerald," I admonished. "We're broken up, remember?"

"Ribbit!"

"Honey, is that you? I was wondering where you were."

I stiffened in shock as my mother came into the foyer. She was one of the last people I expected to see here.

"Mom? What are you doing here? You said you'd never set foot in Rosewater Manor again," I reminded her.

She sighed. "Sage brought me. My sister is very...persuasive. And I have something important to talk to you about." She paused, suddenly noticing the man holding my hand. Her voice turned calculating. "And who is this handsome guy with you?"

I dropped Gabriel's hand like it was on fire.

"This is my, um, friend Gabriel."

"Don't you mean mate?" Pepper offered helpfully from the hallway behind my mother. I shot her a glare.

"Mate? Well, this is quite a development," my mother said in bemusement. "You might as well both come in then. And bring the toad."

When I just stood there staring after my mother, Gabriel swooped down to pick up Gerald in one hand and grabbed my hand with the other. Closing the door behind us, we followed my mother into the parlor. To my surprise, all three of my cousins were there as well as my mother and my Aunt Sage.

"Gabriel, you just met my mother, Pat. This is her sister, my Aunt Sage." I turned to point at my cousins. "These are my cousins, Cami, Pepper, and Meri."

"Nice to meet you all," he said politely.

After giving my Aunt Sage a quick hug, I settled onto a loveseat with Gabriel right next to me, a disgruntled looking Gerald perched on Gabriel's knee.

"Is this the ex?" Aunt Sage asked, nodding at the toad. Or frog, honestly I still wasn't sure.

"Yeah. This is Gerald."

Aunt Sage waved her hand, chanting softly. The air shimmered, and in the blink of an eye, toad Gerald was replaced by human Gerald.

"Dude!" Gabriel yelped. "You're sitting on my junk!"

Gerald leapt off Gabriel's lap like he'd been burned.

"Thank God he was wearing clothes," Gabriel muttered, a flush creeping up his neck. I patted his thigh in comfort, resisting the urge to laugh.

"What the fuck is going on here?" Gerald yelled, turning in a circle around the room as if unsure how he'd gotten there. He looked angrier than I'd ever seen him before, but I guess I couldn't blame him, all things considered. "Where am I? And who are you people?"

Aunt Sage moved closer, her face soft and kind, and placed her hand on his forearm. "It's okay Gerald dear, this was all a weird dream. It's nothing but a dream." Her voice was almost hypnotic.

She nodded to Preston, Meri's mate, who'd just come into the room with Duncan right behind him, then muttered another incantation that made Gerald jolt a little.

"You're going to go with Preston on his private plane and when you wake up, you'll be back in Texas. This was all a dream, you'll remember nothing."

"C'mon Gerald," Preston said, gripping my ex-boyfriend's elbow.

Gerald followed without a word, looking like he was in some kind of trance, while Duncan brought up the rear.

"What'll happen to him?" I asked my aunt.

"He'll wake up at home wondering why he had such a bizarre dream," she explained. "Preston and Duncan will make sure of it."

She returned to her seat and gave my mother a hard look.

"Now that the Gerald situation is fixed, your mother has something important to tell you."

When my mom just sat there staring at the worn throw rug beneath her feet like it held the secret to life, Aunt Sage added sternly, "Tell her, Pat. She deserves to hear the truth."

Gabriel

Jane stiffened beside me, and I wrapped my fingers around hers, offering her my support for whatever was about to happen. It warmed my heart when she leaned into me a bit.

I looked around the parlor, noting the antique furniture and rugs, and walls of shelves filled with leather covered books, family pictures, and various magical paraphernalia. The whole house, well mansion really, was humming with magic. It made my demon side slightly uneasy.

Jane's mother gave her an intense look, took a deep breath, and said, "I never liked being a witch. It always made me feel like a freak. Having power scared me."

"What are you talking about, Mom?" Jane asked. "You said the witchcraft genes skipped you."

"I lied."

Jane gasped in unison with her three cousins.

"But..."

Pat held up her hand. "Please Jane, just let me get this all out, then I promise I'll answer all your questions."

Jane leaned into me a little more, and I released her hand so I could wrap my arm around her shoulder, offering comfort. She snuggled closer.

"Sage and I grew up here, steeped in magic, but I refused to learn the craft. I wanted to be normal. Even among all the shifters around here, I always felt like an anomaly, like I never fit in. Then I went away to college with regular people, with the humans, and I met your father."

Pat's eyes turned sad. "I loved him, but as you know, he was a hard man. Stern. Devout in his Christianity. He caught me doing witchcraft one time – just something minor—and he freaked out. He made me promise I'd never again practice the 'devil's work' as he called it and, well I agreed."

"This sounds like that old TV show with that witch who wiggles her nose," Pepper observed. "She had a husband who hated witchcraft too."

"When you were still just a kid I could tell that you had magic in you," Pat continued. "I knew it would only get stronger when you got older. I was freaking out, thinking that your father would disown you. Disown both of us. I didn't want to lose him, especially not over a power that I didn't like and never wanted. So, I, um, invited Sage to come visit us at our house in Texas. I knew she'd have her grimoire with her, her book of magic spells, and I was determined to find a way to protect you."

She took a shaky breath. "I waited until Sage took Cami to the park and then I found a magic suppression spell and I, well, I deactivated your magic to make you a normal."

"You did what?" Jane gasped in outrage. "How dare you make that decision for me!"

"I did what I thought was best at the time," she whispered, her eyes shiny with tears. "I didn't want you to grow up feeling like a freak the way I did. And I didn't want you to lose your father."

"Mom!"

Pat took a deep breath. "In order to keep the spell strong, I re-did it every year on Samhain, when the veils between the world are the thinnest, and I kept it up even after your father died. But last year on Halloween I'd just met Robert," she looked at me, "that's my new husband. I was totally pre-occupied with him, the way you are when your love is new. And, well, I forgot to re-do the spell, and I haven't thought of it at all since then. I think that over the last year, your magic has been gradually waking up, fighting against the remnants of the spell."

"Oh my God," Jane cried. "I thought I was going crazy the last few months."

"There's more." Pat turned to face Jane's cousin. "Pepper, you were in the room with us when I did the spell. Meri hadn't been born yet and you were just a baby in the crib, that's why you didn't go to the park with your mom and Cami. Anyway, I'm pretty sure that the spell hit you too and that's why you don't have any powers."

"What?!?!?" Pepper jumped up from her seat, her face red with anger. "You took away my magic? Do you have any idea how upsetting it's been to be the only person in my family without any magic powers or psychic skills?"

"I know," Pat said miserably. "I'm so sorry. I had no right to do that to someone else's kid, but I had no idea how to fix you without giving Jane her powers back. I know I was wrong, but I kept this a secret all these years."

"The good news is that now that we know what's happening, Pat and I can do a spell for both of you and remove the effects," Sage said soothingly. "If you have any of my natural magic, Pepper, or your father's psychic skills, it will start to come forth just like Jane's has."

Pepper dropped back into her chair, her two sisters rushing to comfort her. Jane remained silent for a long time before turning to look at me, her face stricken.

"Can you take me home?" she asked quietly. "To your place I mean? I need to get away from here for a while."

"Absolutely." I moved to my feet, grabbing her hand to bring her to standing. My mate needed comfort, and I was glad to be the one to give it to her. My wolf chuffed happily at the idea that she'd trusted us enough to let us take her back to our den.

"I need some time to think," she announced to the group. "I'm going with Gabriel."

"Jane, wait, let's talk about this."

Jane shook her head, sending her mother an angry look.

"No. I'm really mad at you right now, Mom. I'm going to need a bit of time to process this." She looked over to her aunt. "Thanks for your help Aunt Sage. I'll be back tomorrow."

Jane pulled me out of the house, and I led her to my SUV, reaching across her to buckle her in. We drove to the little cabin I was renting just on the outskirts of Greysden, the shifter town where my father and Duncan lived. We were silent the entire ten minute ride.

Pulling into the driveway, I walked around to open the car door fo
Jane. She was sitting completely still, staring straight ahead, eyes dull and
unseeing. I slipped one arm underneath her thighs, the other behind he
back, lifting her into my arms. After kicking the car door closed, I carried
her bridal style into my house, depositing her on the couch. Jane looked
up at me, her eyes vulnerable.

"I can't believe that my mother lied to me my entire life," she
whispered. "I always felt like something wasn't right with me, and now
know why."

When she didn't say anything else, I asked, "When did you last ea
something?"

She frowned. "Last night maybe?"

"Okay I'm going to order us Thai food."

"I'm not hungry."

"You have to eat and besides, my momma always told me there'
nothing you can't heal with hot and spicy Thai soup."

"Demons like Thai food?" she asked in confusion.

"Everyone likes Thai food."

Jane

I had to admit that I did feel better after eating Thai soup, along with some stirred fried chicken and vegetables. I didn't get a lot of Thai food where I lived, and I'd almost forgotten how much I enjoyed it.

As we ate, Gabriel turned the television to some sitcom about nerds living next door to a hot woman. I'd heard of the show but never seen it before. It was a welcome distraction from my turbulent thoughts.

I remembered all the times that I'd visited with my cousins when we were younger, and how Pepper and I always felt left out because Cami had the gift of witchcraft and Meri had psychic skills. Of course, both of them had rather glitchy skills – in fact, Cami had met her mate Stephen after she did a love spell calling him forth for her sister Pepper. And Meri, well I'd heard her skills were getting better, but her visions were...interesting. She could tell you where you'd left your umbrella but rarely anything useful.

Still, Pepper and I had always felt bad about it, like we were defective or something. Glitchy skills were better than nothing, especially in a town that was full of shifters, witches, and other mystical creatures.

I felt Gabriel watching me and turned to meet his eyes. They were glowing red, the way they did when he was turned on. I glanced down and saw the telltale bump of his cock pressing against his pants. Maybe that's what I needed to take my mind off of everything that had happened today.

I leaned forward, meeting his lips with mine. Gabriel let me lead, opening when I licked the seam of his lips. Our tongues met, languorously exploring. I pushed him onto his back, draping myself over him, deepening the kiss.

I still couldn't believe what I'd heard from my mother. I mean, I knew my father was rigid, but I'd never imagined...

Gabriel grabbed my hair, pulling my head away from his.

"I can tell you're not into this," he said. "You're distracted. We don't need to do anything right now."

I flushed with embarrassment. "I'm sorry, I want to, really. I'll just…"

He placed one finger on my lips, the red receding from his eyes. "Do you trust me?"

I met his eyes. "I…yes, I do." It was true, which was totally weird since I'd known the man for two days.

He leveraged up to sitting, then slid off the couch, grabbing my hand to pull me along behind him. "Come on."

I followed him down the hallway to his bedroom.

"Take off your clothes."

His voice was deep and commanding in a way I'd never heard before, and it made me shiver. I debated a sassy response, but I wanted to see where this was going to go. Pulling off my clothes, I dropped them to the floor and stood before him, completely naked. His eyes widened in appreciation, which was great for my ego. At forty, nothing was as firm or high as it used to be, no matter how much I worked out.

"Get on the bed. On your back," he ordered.

I complied, stretching out as instructed with my back pressed against the coolness of the sheets. I heard the closet door open, and he returned holding several belts and what looked like a tie.

"If I do something you don't like or you're feeling uncomfortable, just say 'red' if you want me to stop."

I felt a glimmer of unease. "Wait a minute, if this is some weird billionaire BDSM thing I'm really not down for that. I like my skin unmarked thank you very much."

He smirked. "Relax. I'm not going to hit you with these, I'm just going to help you get out of your head."

Gabriel proceeded to pull my hands over my head, fastening them to the bars of the metal bed frame with one belt. I tugged on my hands, but they were secured pretty well. I didn't want to think about how he knew how to tie someone to the bed. It's not like I thought he was a virgin or something, but just the thought of Gabriel with another woman made me seethe in rage. Oblivious to my inner turmoil, he pulled my legs wide, securing each ankle to the footboard with a belt. I couldn't decide whether I was nervous or completely turned on. Judging by the throbbing between my legs, I was going to go with turned on.

"One more thing," he said.

He pulled the tie around my head, covering my eyes and blocking out the light. I really hoped I wasn't about to be the star attraction on some revenge porn thing. I realized that I knew next to nothing about this man other than what little he'd told me. Suddenly I felt nervous.

"Relax," he commanded. "I won't hurt you. Say 'red' if you don't like something, and I promise that I'll stop. I'll be right back."

What the fuck was happening here? If I woke up without a kidney after the day I'd had, I was going to be really pissed.

I heard his heavy footsteps as he returned to the room, the bed shifting as he sat next to me on the mattress.

"I want you to relax Jane," he said, his voice soft but firm. "Just focus on the sensations, focus on your body."

I jumped as I felt something light touch my skin.

Gabriel chuckled. "It's just a feather. Feel it on your skin. Focus on the touch of the feather."

He ran the feather lightly up my abdomen then around my breast, tickling each nipple before moving lower. The feather circled my belly button before traveling across my pussy lips, then down my inner thigh and back up the other. I could feel my breathing slow as I focused on the slight tickling sensation moving up and down my body.

"Good girl," he growled.

I shouldn't have liked that, but I felt a strong rush of arousal at his words. The feather stopped and I gasped as I felt something cold hit the side of my breast.

"Ice," he whispered. "Focus on the sensations Jane, only the sensations."

Gabriel rubbed the ice cube in circles around one nipple, the cold sensation somewhere in the gray area between painful and arousing. I could feel my nipple hardening. A moment later Gabriel's lips wrapped around the nipple, biting down firmly, and I shrieked.

He moved away immediately. "Are you using your safe word?"

"No," I gasped.

This was the most sensuous experience I'd ever had. My head was completely silent for the first time in forever, the sensations of my body the only thing I could think of.

"God no, don't stop."

I heard him chuckle, then I felt him reach across to grab another ice cube so he could tease the other nipple. My clit was as engorged as my nipples and I moved restlessly on the bed, desperate to relieve the pressure. But Gabriel continued to focus on sliding the ice around my nipple and areola until that one too wound up in his mouth, sharp teeth biting down in a way that almost made me come on the spot.

He moved the ice down, along my ribs to my abdomen, and I began to thrash as much as I could with both my hands and feet restrained. Leaving the remainder of the ice cube dripping over my belly button, Gabriel shifted down the bed.

When I felt the cold ice slip between my folds, I moaned loudly.

"Please Gabriel," I whined. "Please."

"Be a good girl and I'll reward you."

Until this moment, I'd never known that I had a praise kink, but god help me, I did.

The ice slid into my opening, melting immediately against the heat of my molten core, the finger that inserted the ice staying inside me to pump in and out. Then Gabriel sucked my clit into his mouth and that was all it took for me to come so hard I almost blacked out.

Gabriel

ane swore and moaned and possibly spoke in tongues as she came underneath my mouth, thrashing as wildly as she could, given that she was restrained. She was a beautiful sight, her face flushed, her eyes unfocused, her body spread out beneath me like the most sinful of offerings.

I waited until she came down a bit before getting off the bed and shucking my clothes. She lay there boneless as I freed her feet.

"Turn over on your belly," I growled. "Ass up."

She shivered at my intense tone and the primal part of me thrilled. I'd always been a bit dominant in the bedroom, no doubt due to my supernatural side, but I'd never been this demanding before.

She maneuvered onto her abdomen and scooted closer to the headboard until she was able to raise up on her knees. Her arms were stretched over her head, secured to the bed. Her blindfolded face pressed into one arm and her spine arched up to present the round globes of her ass like a gift. I squeezed my erection to keep myself from coming at the sight.

Crawling onto the bed, I moved behind her and stroked her back with one hand. She whimpered.

"You look so beautiful like this, totally at my mercy," I growled, my dual-natured animal close to the surface. I couldn't say whether it was my wolf or my demon, maybe both.

I gripped her ass, one cheek in each hand and squeezed her hard. She gasped, but pushed back against me, letting me know she enjoyed a bit of pain. Without warning, I shoved myself deep inside her. Her entrance was wet, but I was a big guy, so it was still a little tight.

I smacked her ass cheek with one hand. "Relax."

She shuddered but I felt her internal muscles loosen. I smacked her ass again and she gave me another one of those sexy little whimpers. "Good girl."

I had no idea where this was all coming from. I'd never talked to a woman like this before in my life, but somehow with Jane, it felt right.

I pulled back until just the tip of my cock remained inside her, then shoved forward roughly again. I saw her fingers wrap around the bed post, wrists still restrained by my belt, and she pushed back against me, letting me know she wanted more. But I needed to hear it.

"Do you want more?" I growled. "You want me to wreck your sweet pussy with my giant cock?"

She nodded, and I slapped her ass again, the cracking sound loud in the quiet of the room.

"I didn't hear you."

"Gabriel," she gasped. "Please. Fuck me now. Please!"

"Good girl," I said again, and the squeezing of her internal muscles let me know how much she liked to be praised.

I set a brutal pace, gripping her hips as I pounded into her from behind. She slid up the bed with each stroke, only her grip on the headboard keeping me from fucking her right through the wall. The animal side of me loved this. It was dirty and raw and...perfect.

"I need you to come Jane," I ordered. I smacked her ass again. "Come now!"

Her pussy was like a vise as she came again, bucking and shaking beneath me with the force of her orgasm. I lowered myself over her back, trapping her beneath me, surrounding her, and that was all it took for me to lose the tenuous control I had on myself.

"Mate!" I roared as I emptied myself into her, coming longer and harder than I had in my life.

I lowered my mouth to her shoulder, compelled to bite her again to reconfirm my possession. The bite prolonged her orgasm, which impossibly prolonged mine. Her knees collapsed, causing me to drop on top of her until I came back into my body long enough to pull out.

I reached up to free her wrists, turning her into my embrace. She draped herself over me like I was a life sized pillow, and we fell asleep wrapped in each other's arms.

To my shock, we both slept through the night. I awoke just after six, feeling the pressing need of nature's call, and when I returned to the bedroom, Jane was awake, sitting up and leaning against the pillows, looking rumpled and sexy as hell.

"Good morning, Mate."

"Good morning," she said, her voice sounding uncertain. "Sorry I fell asleep here."

"I'm not. If I have my way, you'll sleep here next to me every night for the rest of your life."

Her eyes widened, and I could practically see her building up walls around her. She slid off the bed. "I need to go to the bathroom."

She stood up, beautifully naked, and grabbed her clothes. Clutching them to her chest, she raced past me to the bathroom across the hall. I sighed and went into the kitchen to make coffee. I had a feeling I was going to need it.

Jane came out a few minutes later and without a word, I handed her a cup of coffee. She inhaled deeply. "Mmm."

"Sorry I don't have any cream, but I might have some sugar somewhere."

"No, this is great. I prefer my coffee black. Thanks."

"Are you hungry?" I asked her. "I'm sorry, but I don't really have anything for breakfast other than cereal and pop tarts."

She giggled, and the sound soothed something deep inside me.

"Cereal and pop tarts? What are you, in college?"

I shook my head. "I usually pick something up on my way to work."

Her eyes widened. "Oh god, I don't even know what you do for a living."

"I work in construction," I said quickly. "There's a wolf shifter named Stuart Grey who runs a contracting company here in town. We do mostly remodeling work."

She nodded. "I guess that explains why you're so fit."

"That and the shifter genes," I told her. "It's hit or miss with the demon side, but the wolves are always muscular with low body fat."

I wanted to slap myself as soon as the words were out of my mouth. I felt nervous, but I wasn't sure why.

"What about you?"

"Are you asking me about my body fat percentage?" she asked incredulously.

To my horror, I started to blush.

"No! I meant to ask about your job."

"Oh. Yeah. I'm an office manager. Nothing exciting."

We stared at each other for a long moment, the silence becoming awkward. Jane straightened her spine before she spoke again.

"Look, Gabriel, we need to talk."

Oh yeah, that was why I was nervous. Never in the history of relationships had anything good come out of a woman telling a man they needed to talk. I could sense what was coming, and so could my inner wolf. He was whining and scratching inside me. I got my emotional side from the wolf in me. Demons tended to be a bit calmer and more strategic, unless they were angry, then all bets were off.

I suppressed a sigh. "Shall we sit down?"

Jane

I sat across the kitchen table and looked at Gabriel. He looked freaking delicious with his hair rumpled and his jaw covered in scruff. I had an image of that scruff scraping against my inner thighs and stuffed it down. We'd had sex four times in the twenty-four hours between the Halloween party and last night. As much as I'd loved it, I wasn't used to having such rough, intense sex, and things were a little sore down there. Besides, I needed to focus on the things I wanted to say to him.

I looked around the kitchen to distract myself. It was a little dated, but neat as a pin. The whole house was adorable. I wondered idly if he owned or rented, then reminded myself to focus on the matter at hand, not daydream about moving in here with him.

"First, I want to tell you how much I appreciate what you did last night. Giving me a place to get away, feeding me, and well, everything that came after. I mean, it was incredible. That was the single most hottest sexual experience I've ever had, if I'm being honest."

It had also helped me get out of my head and settle my emotions, though I didn't share that part.

Gabriel raised his eyebrows at me, his expression stricken, as if he knew what was coming. "But?"

"But we've only known each other two days."

"Today's technically the third day," he protested.

I rolled my eyes.

"I came here to figure out what was going on with me, and in two, sorry three days, I have sex with a stranger four times in like twenty-four hours, watch my ex get turned back into a human, and then I find out my entire life was a lie. It's a lot to process."

He nodded. "Yeah. But there's one very important thing you need to know before you make any decisions. I love you."

I gasped. "You can't love me. It's too fast. I mean, I know you shifters work fast but this is ridiculous."

"Except my demon side is very pragmatic and still loves you, no matter how long it's been. Don't you feel it, Jane? It's like we've known each other our whole lives. We just...we just fit."

God, he was right, but I was too muddled to deal with this right now. I was reeling. My entire life and everything I'd thought I'd known about myself had changed since I drove into Greysden a couple of days ago. It was a lot to deal with.

"I'm sorry Gabriel, I don't want to hurt you, I swear I don't, but I need some time. I need to process everything that's happened. And I need to do it alone."

"What are you saying?" he asked, his face stricken.

"I'm going back to Texas." I held up my hand as he hissed out a breath. "We can talk or video chat or whatever if you want, but I don't know if I can do this with you, at least not right now. I'm sorry, really I am, but I need some time to figure out what I'm going to do with my life now. Everything's changed in an instant."

I heard a horn sound outside and stood up. "That's Pepper."

Walking around the table, I pressed a kiss on his cheek. He spun his head, catching my lips with his. His kiss was hard and full of emotion and when I finally pulled away, we were both panting for breath and his eyes were glowing red with his demon.

"Please come back to me Jane. Or I'll come to you. Just don't..." his voice broke along with my heart. "Don't give up on us."

"I left my number on the nightstand. Text me so I have your number and I'll let you know when I get home to Texas."

I ran out of the room without looking back, knowing that if I did, I would never leave him. I waited until I was safely in Pepper's car before I let the tears fall.

"Are you all right?" she asked.

"Yeah," I sniffed. "I'm just so confused about everything that's happened in the last few days."

"You're going back to Texas, aren't you?"

"How did you know?"

"I know you, cousin. You want to go back to your house and lick your wounds and analyze everything that happened and try to make sense of it."

"Do you blame me?"

She shook her head. "Not at all. I'm still reeling from finding out what your mom did. I mean, spending our whole lives thinking we're the non-magical misfits of the family and then learning it was all a spell? It's been, what, thirty-five years since this happened? I could kill your mom."

"Same. What happened after I left? I'm sorry I took off, but I just needed to get out of there before I exploded."

"Oh I get it, believe me. After you left, Aunt Pat and my mom had a huge blow-up. You know my mom doesn't usually get mad, she's always all 'blessed be' and 'let karma handle it' but she was livid that your mom not only fucked with you, but with me too. I think Mom felt bad that she never figured it out, and that made her even angrier. Anyway, words were exchanged, and your mom left in a self-righteous huff on her way back to Florida. She says to call her when you want to talk."

"Like that's going to happen any time soon."

"Well, my mom reversed the spell for both of us, so whatever natural powers we have should be coming out over the next few months."

"I'm glad you got your powers Pepper, I know you always wanted them."

"I'm glad too," she said. "For both of us. I can't wait to see what we can do when the spell wears off."

"Hey, I'm starving. Do you want to grab breakfast with me before I leave?"

Pepper perked up. "As long as we're in Greysden, let's go to the Xenakis Diner. Those badger shifters are nosy as hell, but they make a mean breakfast."

Two hours later I was on the road, my furry black Familiar sitting on the passenger seat giving me the stink eye.

"Look cat, I know you think I should stay in Colorado, but I need some time to regroup."

"Meow."

"I guess I should give you a name if you're going to stick around. How about Midnight?"

"Meow."

"Yeah, I didn't like that either, it's so cliché. I'll give it some more thought."

"Meow."

"Can you quit bringing up Gabriel? I'm not saying I'll never come back, I'm just saying I need some time to think. Get off my back."

"Meow."

Gabriel

"How long is this 'woe is me' act going to go on?"

I looked over at my brother from my place at the bar. Murphy's was hopping, and the wolf shifter behind the bar hadn't stopped moving all night. Not that I cared about anything but getting drunk.

"Hey Marie," Duncan called to the bartender. He seemed to know every single person living in this town. "Can I get a beer please?"

"Sure thing Duncan."

The bartender slid my brother a drink and Duncan gave her a charming smile. "Thanks, Darling."

We both turned as a low growl came from the other side of the bar. Marie rolled her eyes at the big shifter who looked like he wanted to rip Duncan's arms off and feed them to the customers.

"Relax Gentle Ben," Marie called back pointedly. "I've known Duncan for years. He knows I have a mate." She added under her breath, "Stupid bears."

Duncan turned his attention back to me. "Well?"

"Well, what?" I asked belligerently.

It's possible that I was the tiniest bit drunk. As a shifter-demon hybrid, I had a great metabolism, and it was really hard to get drunk. But I'd learned over the years that rapid drinking of shifter-made alcohol, which was stronger than regular alcohol, was the key to taking the edge off. And I'd been taking the edge off for hours now, so I was good and drunk.

"Are you going to spend the rest of your life drinking in this damn bar, or are you going to go get your mate?"

"She said she needs time," I grumbled.

"She's had time."

"It's only been three days since she left."

Three days since I woke up with her in my arms only to have Jane rip my heart out with her bare hands. Not that I shared that part with my brother.

Duncan waved his hand dismissively. "Three days in human time is a lifetime to shifters."

I lowered my head to the bar. The last three days had been exceedingly long. I couldn't sleep, couldn't concentrate on work, couldn't do anything but think of Jane racing out of my kitchen and out of my life. Meanwhile my demon was giving me the silent treatment and my wolf was full-on belligerent, demanding that we go find our mate and drag her home to the den.

"I don't know what to do," I whispered. "I love her so much."

Duncan patted me on the back. "You're going to finish your beer, go home and sober up, then in the morning you're going to go to Texas and get your mate," he instructed. "Also, I'd strongly recommend a shower."

The next morning, I got up early and made the seven-hour drive to Amarillo. I felt calm and focused the entire trip, a sure sign I was doing the right thing. Duncan had gotten Jane's address from her cousin Meri after extracting a promise that she wouldn't tell Jane I was surprising her. I just hoped it was a good surprise.

It was mid-afternoon when I drove up to the ranch house where Jane lived. I pulled into the driveway, looking around curiously. It was a cute neighborhood, a little cookie cutter though. I suddenly realized that I had no idea what Jane's schedule was. She'd mentioned that she was an office manager, so I assumed that meant she worked Monday through Friday. Since today was Saturday, I hoped that meant she would be home.

"Meow."

I looked down to see Jane's Familiar on the porch watching me.

"Hey cat, is your friend home?"

When the cat continued to stare at me, I nutted up and pressed the doorbell. A few minutes later, Jane opened the door and my heart stuttered. Even dressed casually in faded jeans and a tee shirt with no make-up at all she was so beautiful. Everything inside me settled for the first time since she'd left me in Greysden.

"Hi."

She stared at me in surprise. "Gabriel. What are you doing here?"

"I missed you. Can I come in?"

My mate opened the door wider, and I followed her into the house, looking around curiously. "Nice place."

Jane turned around, her mouth open to ask me a question, but whatever it was that she was going to say was forgotten as we flew towards each other. I pulled her into my arms, squeezing her close as if that would keep her from getting away again, and lowered my mouth to hers.

The kiss was immediately red hot, and Jane raised her hands to stroke my horns, instantly making me so hard that my cock was damn near punching through my pants. I broke away and walked us towards the couch.

I didn't think, I just acted as I whipped her jeans down her hips and ripped off her underwear with my claws. Jane gasped but didn't protest. I swung her around to lean over the arm of the couch. She braced her hands on the seat cushion as I freed my cock and plunged into her roughly, desperate to claim her again. We both groaned as I bottomed out deep inside her, her inner muscles squeezing around me.

Gripping her hips, I began pounding into her. There was no foreplay, no finesse, just me rutting into her like the animal I was.

"Don't." Pound.

"Ever." Pound.

"Leave me." Pound.

"Again."

"Gabriel," she gasped. "Oh my God!"

I lowered myself over her back and gripped her shoulder between my teeth, breaking the skin and marking her again as if it would hold her to me better than the first time I did it. As soon as I felt her blood in my mouth she came with a long wail, and I was right behind her. I surged into her, pumping into her in long spurts until I was totally spent.

My knees buckled as I finished, and I slid to the floor, my naked ass on the hardwood. Jane turned and lowered herself to sit on my lap.

"Wow, you really know how to greet a girl," she teased.

I slipped my finger underneath her chin so that she turned her head to meet my gaze.

"I'm moving here."

"What?"

"I'm moving to Texas. I want to be with you Jane, whatever it takes."

At her sharp intake of breath, I hastened to add, "I don't expect to live here with you. Not yet. I'll get a place nearby so we can spend time together and get to know each other better. We can take all the time you need to see that I mean it when I say that I love you. I just need you to give me a chance."

"Well, you moving down here is going to be a huge problem."

My heart thudded to a stop. Was my mate really going to continue to reject me, even after that enthusiastic greeting?

"Why can't I move to Amarillo to be with you?" I asked, hearing my miserable tone.

We both jumped as the doorbell rang.

"Because I'm moving to Colorado to be with you instead."

Jane rose to her feet, then reached down to offer me her hand. "Now get your pants on. That's my realtor."

I grabbed her hand, my heart beating so hard I could hear it in my ears.

"You're moving to Colorado? To be with me? Really?"

She nodded. "I love you Gabriel, and I want to spend the rest of my life with you."

"Really?" I asked again, afraid it was all just a dream.

"Really."

"In that case, let's get this house on the market, love. I can't wait to get you home."

Epilogue – Jane

One year later...

"Noooo!!!"

The high-pitched sound was enough to shatter glass. Or my eardrums anyway.

"Why did I let you talk me into this?" I groaned, sending a frustrated look towards my husband.

"You said you always wanted kids," Gabriel reminded me. "And the universe delivered."

"Meow."

I glared at my Familiar. "I don't need you piling onto me, Ebony!"

"Mama. Mama. Mama. Maaamaaa!"

I took a deep breath before turning to look at our four-year-old son Roger. He was half demon, half jaguar shifter, and fully mischievous. We'd adopted him and his three-year-old sister Rachel, a full demon as far as we could tell. We hadn't planned to have kids, given that I was already in my forties, but when we learned that their mother, a distant cousin of Gabriel's on his mother's side, had died a year ago, leaving the kids in foster care up in New Jersey, we knew we had to help.

We'd learned that the kids had been in and out of foster care ever while their mother was alive, due to the drug addiction that had eventually killed her. No one knew who the kids' fathers were, probably not even their mother.

Roger and Rachel had come to live with us about six months ago and the adoption had been finalized last week. That was much faster than these things usually happened, but Duncan's boss Preston was a well-connected billionaire who'd been able to fast track the process for us. The last thing anyone wanted was for the kids to start shifting into their other forms while living in a human foster home. While shifters weren't in hiding, most humans were oblivious to things they didn't understand, like shifters and demons, and everyone preferred it that way.

"Rachel won't give me her candy!" Roger told me, clearly outraged.

"That's her candy," I reminded him. "She trick-or-treated for it just like you did for yours. Why don't you get one piece of your own candy?"

"Ebony took it?" Roger's voice was uncertain, as if he didn't believe his own lie.

Gabriel raised his eyebrows, adopting what I thought of as his 'stern dad' voice. A voice I loved to hear when we were all alone.

"Are you lying Roger?"

"No," Roger said, nodding. I tried not to laugh.

"I want you to run five laps around the yard and think about your answer some more," Gabriel ordered.

It was hardly a punishment. Roger loved to run. But giving him something to channel his excess energy was always a good plan. Our kids had come to us with a lot of trauma from their time in foster care, and whatever they'd experienced with their mother, but they were slowly healing here in our home.

Gabriel put his arm around me as we watched Roger run. I leaned into him, pondering how much my life had changed in the past year.

Last Halloween I was forty, living alone, and trying to figure out how I'd turned my pesty ex-boyfriend into a toad. Now I was married and mated, the mother of two rambunctious kids, and living in the magical town of Greysden Colorado with the love of my life.

I had also fully embraced my witch side, reading up on the history of witchcraft and taking lessons from my Aunt Sage. I'd never be as powerful as she was, but my skills were coming along, and so were Pepper's, to her immense relief.

I'd found a job here in Greysden and moved in with Gabriel. We'd both lived alone for way too many years to have an easy transition, but we'd worked things out together, with lots of make-up sex. Despite our fast start, we'd built a relationship of trust, respect, and most importantly, love. I really couldn't complain about anything.

"Nooooooo!"

Except my daughter's piercing scream, that is.

"Roger, keep running and leave your sister alone!" Gabriel ordered.

My mate and I shared a smile as our son resumed his joyful running around the yard. Last Halloween had been a surprise, but this year the surprise was how we'd made it so long without each other.

I reached up and wrapped one hand around Gabriel's left horn, stroking it in the way that I know made him get hard in under a minute. He groaned.

"Hey there, handsome. As soon as these kids are asleep, how about we recreate our first time in the closet for old time's sake?"

My husband gave me a smile that was pure sin.

"It's a date."

***

You can read about Jane's cousins, the Rosewater Sisters, in the Magical Midlife Series. Cami is the first to find her true love, kind of, in Love Potion[1], available everywhere.

And remember the bartender Marie who's mated to a bear named Ben? You can read their story in Cocktail Wolf[2], available everywhere now.

If you liked this book, please show me some love, and leave a review. Good reviews are like puppies, they make everyone feel happy.

Keep reading for a special excerpt from "Wolf Doctor[3]".

---

1. https://books2read.com/u/4X6pN7

2.   https://books2read.com/u/baGvZ6

3.   https://books2read.com/u/4AOXXK

Special Preview

Wolf Doctor by Rose Bak

Twilight. Colt's favorite time of the day.

Stripping off his clothes, he took a deep breath, inhaling the scents on the air. He broke into a run and felt his body change mid-stride. In less than thirty seconds he had transformed from man to wolf.

Muscles and bone lengthening as gray hair sprouted all over his body, almost white in some places. His sharp canine teeth extended from his thickening jaw. He felt his tail grow behind him and he wagged it happily from side to side as he increased his pace, moving so fast his paws seemed to barely touch the ground.

Colt's senses were immediately heightened. His vision was sharper, his ears taking in even the softest sound, and his nose twitched with the wonderful scents of the pristine forest.

He headed through the woods, exhilarating in the feeling of free movement. His wolf loved to run. He hadn't shifted in almost a week. Too long. He needed this. He needed to shift and let his wolf run as much as he needed oxygen or food.

Speaking of food, he could use a snack. He scented a group of hares a mile away and headed in that direction at a gallop. His paws ate up the ground as he tracked the smaller beasts, stopping occasionally to sniff the ground and pick up their trail.

There, up ahead, he saw a flash of fur. He moved quickly, ears pinned back, as his wolf took over, the ultimate predator.

He could smell the fear on the hare as it took off, running for its life. Colt pulled his gums back in a canine smile. He loved the chase. The harder the capture, the better it tasted.

He sped up, following the hare instinctively as it took a sharp turn to the side. He pounced, leaping after the hare. Suddenly his feet hit air. And then he was falling. Fast.

Oh crap. He had overshot and gone right over the edge of the bluff. He could practically feel the stupid hare laughing at him as he tumbled down the embankment, scrambling but unable to stop his downward momentum.

He whined as his body hit the road below with a heavy thump.

Before he could recover he heard the squealing of brakes and suddenly he was airborne again. He landed on the asphalt a second time, feeling bones breaking and muscles tearing. He smelled the scent of his own blood and dimly heard voices as he struggled to stay conscious.

"Oh my god Dennis, you hit that poor dog!" The woman sounded upset.

"I'm not sure that it's a dog Sandy, it might be a wolf," someone, presumably Dennis, responded.

Not a dog, his wolf snipped in his head, clearly offended.

Really, that's your top worry right now? he asked his wolf.

Like all shifters, Colt shared space in his mind with his animal. He and his wolf shared not only the same body, but also the same consciousness.

He noted dimly that the humans who had hit him had exited their truck and were watching him cautiously from where they had stopped. He thought about getting up and whined again. The pain was terrible. It was impossible to move.

"He's bleeding and he's in pain," Sandy said, her voice sounding closer. "We have to get him to the animal hospital."

"There's no way he's going to survive," Dennis answered. "Let me get my shotgun out of the truck and I'll put the poor thing out of his misery."

Colt lifted his head in alarm, although it cost him dearly. He made eye contact with the woman, trying to communicate with her. He tried to make himself look sad and unthreatening. He did not want to die on the side of the road, and he definitely did not want to be put down by some random human with a shotgun. With his luck the guy would be a bad shot and make his injuries even worse.

"NO," Sandy said firmly. "You are not shooting him Dennis. Get the tarp. We'll put him in the back and drive him to the vet."

"He's a wounded animal Sandy," Dennis argued. "He may attack us, especially if he is a wolf."

Sandy continued to hold Colt's gaze. "No, he won't," she replied. "Come on, let's get him some help."

Colt passed out, not knowing who would win their argument. He just hoped it was Sandy.

He did not feel the couple cautiously wrapping him in a tarp and dragging him up into the back of their pick-up. He didn't feel himself sliding around in the truck bed as they raced to the animal hospital. He didn't hear the people loading him onto a gurney and wheeling his large body into the hospital. Both his body and his mind were completely shut down now, blissfully blocking the pain.

Then he felt it. A jolt of happiness and peace.

He opened his eyes, staring through the pain as an angel looked down at him. The overhead light glowed behind her like a halo. Thick brown hair framed her beautiful face. Her eyes were deep brown and impossibly kind.

"What happened?" his angel asked. Her voice made him feel calm. She seemed familiar.

"I think he took a header off a cliff. I think he came rolling down from up above. Suddenly there he was, falling onto the road right in front of us," Dennis explained. "Before I could stop, I hit him with my truck. I didn't do it on purpose, he seemed to come out of nowhere."

The angel's hand dropped gently to his head, rubbing him softly between his ears. He closed his eyes again, pressing against the warmth of her hand and whining softly. He had one thought before he passed out again. *Mate!*

***

For more of Colt's story, check out "Wolf Doctor" by Rose Bak. Available at select online retailers[1].

---

1. *https://books2read.com/u/4AOXXK*

Other Books by Rose Bak

Bite-Sized Shifters Paranormal Romance Series
Long Distance Wolf
Wolf Doctor
Kat's Dog
Designer Wolf
Wolf Sheriff
Cocktail Wolf
Second Chance Wolf
Runaway Wolf
Magical Midlife Series
Love Potion
Psychic Flashes
Halloween Surprise
Giant Love
Holidays with the Shifters Series
Santa's Claws
Bear Humbug
Jingle Bear
Silver Paws
Joy to the Wolf
Lion's Heart
Loving the Holidays Contemporary Romance Series
Dating Santa
New Year's Steve
Independence Dave
Comfort & Joy
Faking It with the Detective
Dropping the Ball
Boozy Book Club Series
Beach Reads

Bubbly & Billionaires
Martinis & Mysteries
Bourbon & Bikers
Midlife Madness
Extra Innings
The Good with Numbers Holiday Romance Series
Love Unmasked
The Thanksgiving Scrooge
Maid for Christmas
Countdown to Love
Valentine's Lottery
Christmas Angel
The Oliver Boys Band Contemporary Romance Series
Until You Came Along
Rock Star Teacher
Rock Star Writer
Rock Star Neighbor
Rock Star Lawyer
The Midlife Crisis Contemporary Romance Series
Summer Wedding
Roasting with Rob
Christmas Punch
Reunited Contemporary Romance Series
Together Again
Finding My Baby
King of the Reunion
The Diamond Bay Contemporary Romance Series
Brand New Penny
Fresh as a Daisy
Right as Rain
Standalones
Beach Wedding

Jessie's Girl

Non-fiction

What to Do If You Find a Cougar in Your Living Room: Self-Care in an Uncaring World

It's All About Relationships: Reflections on Love, Friendship, and Connection

Catch up with these and other stories coming soon at bit.ly/AuthorRoseBak.

Join my newsletter for more information[1] or follow my author page on your favorite retailer.

---

1. *https://storyoriginapp.com/giveaways/62ee758e-068f-11eb-904e-c373f6014fe1*

About the Author

Rose Bak has been obsessed with books since she got her first library card at age five. She is a passionate reader with an e-reader bursting with thousands of beloved books.

Although Rose enjoys writing both fiction and nonfiction, romance novels have always been her favorite guilty pleasure, both as a reader and an author. Rose's contemporary romance books focus on strong female characters over thirty-five and the alpha males who love them. Expect a lot of steam, a little bit of snark, and a guaranteed happily ever after.

Rose lives in the Pacific Northwest with her family, and special needs dogs. In addition to writing, she also teaches accessible yoga and loves music. Sadly, she has absolutely no musical talent, so she mostly sings in the shower.

Please sign up for the Rose Bak Romance newsletter at bit.ly/rosebaknewsletter[1] to get a free book and keep up to date on all the latest news, sales, and free offerings.

You can also follow Rose on Facebook[2], Instagram[3], Twitter[4], Goodreads[5], or Bookbub[6].

---

1. https://storyoriginapp.com/giveaways/ba6caac0-d4f9-11ed-80b7-073007e1a152
2. https://www.facebook.com/AuthorRoseBak
3. https://www.instagram.com/authorrosebak/
4. https://twitter.com/AuthorRoseBak
5. https://www.goodreads.com/authorrosebak
6. https://www.bookbub.com/authors/rose-bak

Don't miss out!

Visit the website below and you can sign up to receive emails whenever Rose Bak publishes a new book. There's no charge and no obligation.

https://books2read.com/r/B-A-VATM-MBVBC

BOOKS2READ

Connecting independent readers to independent writers.

Did you love *Halloween Surprise*? Then you should read *Love Potion*[7] by Rose Bak!

[8]

The love spell worked…on the wrong sister!When her sister begs her to do a love spell to attract her true mate, Cami is hesitant. Her magic is glitchy on a good day. But what's the harm of trying? To everyone's shock, the spell manifests exactly the man they hoped for, except for one problem…he's in love with Cami, not her sister.Shapeshifter Stephen doesn't believe in magic, but he does believe in fate. His wolf knows the truth: Cami is his true mate, the one he's destined to be together with forever. If only Cami could forget about the spell and listen to her heart…"Love Potion" is book one in the Magical Midlife Romance series. This steamy opposites attract novella includes matchmaking sisters, a wolf shifter who's found his fated mate, and a little touch of magic

---

7. https://books2read.com/u/4X6pN7

8. https://books2read.com/u/4X6pN7

leading to a sweet happily ever after. Download this instalove romantic comedy today!

Read more at https://rosebakenterprises.com/.